THE VIOLENCE OF FIRE

ABIGAIL GRIMES

THE VIOLENCE OF FIRE

The Violence of Fire/ Abigail Grimes -- 1st ed.

abigailgrimes.com

ISBN-13: 978-1-9990069-3-8

Follow Abigail Grimes on
Instagram & Twitter
@writtenbygrimes

Dedication

To my parents, Sandra and Godfrey.

Thank you for, well, everything.

And I will show you something different from either

Your shadow in the morning striding behind you

Or your shadow at evening rising to meet you

I will show you fear in a handful of dust

-T.S. Eliot, The Waste Land

THE VIOLENCE OF FIRE

The Violence of Fire

Chapter One

Night had fallen on the cool September day. Gazing out her office window, she watched the city's skyline blink to life. Stretching in her high back leather chair, she begins to pack up her desk. Piling the memos and affidavits chaotically on the corner of her desk, she makes a note that she has to do better at keeping her space more organized. Organization is the tell of a chaotic mind. Is that the saying?

Regardless, she knew that she understood her filing system. As did her assistant, and really, who else needed to understand it? She wrote her assistant a note on a sticky pad requesting that he order new sticky pads and turned off the light on her desk. Slipping on her heels, she stood to face the large bank of windows. Taking in the cityscape once more, she plucked her purse from the sofa in her office, grabbed her blazer from the antique coat rack, and walked out the door.

The echo of her heels filled the main lobby. It was very late. Brianne Wagner usually wasn't the last to leave the office, but with the deposition of her major client the following afternoon, she wanted to ensure she was prepared.

She had sent her assistant, Phillip Cobb, out at 7 o'clock to grab some dinner for the two of them, but when he returned Brianne insisted that he go home to his family. A father of two young children did not need to spend the night in the office waiting for her to send him something to research or type. What couldn't be finished that evening would have to wait until the morning, and she considered herself a fair boss in that respect.

She took the elevator to the underground parking garage and got into her sedan. Driving up the three levels to the ground, she swiped her pass and exited the garage into the waiting arms of the city.

Brianne loved the night. There was an energy to everything at night. It was almost electric. From the way the streetlights lit up the roadway to the excited energy of the passersby as they hustled to their destinations. Were they heading to the movies? Going to a pub with friends? Stopped at an intersection, she smiled as she watched a striking young man holding the door for an equally striking young man. Watching the young couple, she pondered if they were on a date. The city was alive on a Thursday.

Phillip had stood in the shadow of the garage and watched Brianne as she walked to her car. She was beautiful and elegant. But she was also clumsy and a terrible slob. She never straightened her desk before she left for the evening, and that was something that Phillip could not abide. He would have to go to the office early tomorrow to attend to the mess she left behind.

She drove him crazy.

Brianne had told him to go home, but he couldn't. Not yet. He had to watch to make sure she was on her way first. So, there he remained, in the shadows. When she joined the firm six years ago, his whole world had changed. This brilliant creature, this dominant, intelligent woman. She brought with her a fresh attitude to their stuffy boy's club, and the change in the office was almost immediate.

The other women in the office no longer felt they had to allow themselves to be subjected to their boss, Charles', leering and nauseating flirtations. Brianne seemed to be immune to him and his advances. She peeled away the aura of his influence and revealed that subjecting oneself to his lechery was not the hurdle one had to overcome to advance their career.

There was now someone with influence in the office who saw merit, not the length of one's skirt. It had earned her a certain quiet notoriety among staff, and Phillip quickly became one of her biggest fans. He had no love lost for Charles. In the three years Phillip had worked under Charles he watched a seemingly endless parade of women pass through his office door, who had little if anything to do with the legal profession. Though, he had to admit, the man's appetite was admirable. Then Brianne came on board, and while she was below him, she never allowed herself to be beneath him.

Phillip admired her resolve, how she dealt with his advances. There was something about her that Charles wanted and could never get. And Charles was a man who could have anything. It made the mystery of Brianne even more delicious.

Charles, always one to work the angles, assigned Phillip to her, but as Charles would learn, Phillip was far more interested in making Brianne happy than he was plying her for Charles' eventual accosting. And it was not long before a frustrated Charles set his sights on his new, young assistant, leaving Phillip to appreciate Brianne in his own way.

The Violence of Fire

Over the next six years, Phillip and Brianne worked together, and the two of them developed a strong relationship. She trusted him and he her. And well she should. He took care of everything for her. He often wondered what she would do if he were gone. She would be helpless; he was so integral to her life.

He typed her memos, he read and responded to her emails, he picked up her laundry from the cleaners, brought her breakfast in the morning, they shared late dinners. There wasn't another person in the world he felt closer to, and that included his wife. He could read her mind, and he could anticipate her needs.

He knew that she needed him.

As he stood in the shadow, he thought about her and all the things about her that drove him so crazy. Her messy desk, the way she tapped on the keyboard when she was developing an argument. The way her hair fell forward and hid her eyes when she concentrated over a file. The curve of her neck, the swell of her breast beneath her blouse, the cleft behind her knee. Did she really think that he didn't notice? He tried his best to remain under control in the office, but she taunted him. She knew just what she was doing to him.

Straining to keep his composure, to not step out of the shadows after her as she drove away, he knew he had to attend to his pressing need. Phillip lit a cigarette, the flash of flame and glow of the embers casting his face in a moment of disjointed light and shadow. Phillip got into his car and drove into the innocent night seeking reprieve.

Chapter Two

Though she loved the excitement of the city, Brianne also loved the quiet and stillness of the countryside. She turned onto the 401 and pointed her car east. She would be home in an hour. The commute was extensive, but to her mind, it was worth the reward. She lived on a five-acre parcel of land surrounded by woodlands. Her 500-meter length driveway was bisected by a creek that led to a private pond. Coming home to a wood fire burning in the parlor was one of her life's greatest pleasures. The dichotomy of her love for both the country and the city was always a comical topic for discussion among her colleagues who believed that if one loved the city, then one could not also love the country.

A carpenter by trade, Hugo Wagner lived in a house that had a workshop in the back and lots of room for his dog to run — having grown up on a farm he loved the solitude and honesty of country living. Convincing Brianne to move in with him hadn't been as daunting a task as he originally thought. Having met the up and coming lawyer in a downtown nightclub several years prior, he knew she loved the city and the nightlife; all of life's amenities and desires a mere stone's throw away. But they had fallen in love, and they soon came to realize that they could have both the excitement and the quiet. Hugo built Brianne a beautiful desk from a fallen walnut oak on the property and presented it to her one Christmas early in their courtship. They spent the following weeks transforming the den off the parlor into her own private office and by April Brianne had moved into the grey farmhouse.

Greeted at the door with a glass of Riesling, Hugo joined her, and they caught up on the goings-on of each other's day. Listening to the timbre of his voice, Brianna sunk deeper into his arms. They made love before the roaring fire, the heat of the flames licking their bodies. When morning broke, the tenderness of the night in the past, they rushed about the house to prepare for the day that lay ahead.

Chapter Three

Brianne arrived at her office at 9:30 am. Passing her assistant's desk, she picked up her coffee and danish and made her way into the conference room. Her boss, Charles Tillerson, stood at the windows gazing down over the city.

"Your client called and wants to move up the deposition." Turning from the window to face her, she could see that he was not impressed. "If you can move it up with opposing counsel, work it out. The sooner you deal with him, the sooner he is out of our lives."

With that, Charles left her alone in the conference room.

Brianne rolled her eyes. Dealing with Charles was exhausting. He was a demanding boss, and she had no issue with that. It was the underlying sexual predatory nature of his demands that she could not stomach. He was a snake, but at least he was her snake, and as long as she was making him money, he pretty much left her alone. Phillip had run that interference fairly well when she first started there, and now, aside from his occasional bawdy talk or random acts of testosterone-fueled barking, he allowed her to work without interruption.

But here it was, moments before their star divorcée was to blow through their doors for the third time since Brianne had worked there--Charles' barely contained tantrum and his tiresome unimpressed face.

Difficult clients were just that, difficult. But none were more so than one who refused to pay on time, do what he is told and co-operate with his own lawyers. He had not wanted to give any concessions, but that was not uncommon in the divorce proceedings of wealthy clients. He was trying to make it as uncomfortable as possible for his wife to move on. And by doing so, he made it very difficult to work with him as he did not adhere to any particular legal strategy set out for him. He wanted to hurt her because she had hurt him, and he didn't care much about how he accomplished his goal.

Brianne sighed and sat down. She did not want to go out of her way for this particular client, but he was a big fish for this firm.

She buzzed Phillip's desk to ask him to give her counsel's number, but he did not answer.

After a brief search for Phillip, whom she could not locate, then the telephone number, Brianne contacted counsel for the opposing party only to learn that they were not amenable to changing the time of the deposition.

Their client, the most recent, Former Mrs. Big Fish, would arrive at 2:00 pm as scheduled. Apparently, she wasn't willing to make any concessions either.

Phillip had arrived in the conference room while Brianne was on the phone and he offered to advise their client to arrive at two as agreed so that Brianne could prepare in her office. She agreed, and as she passed by him she smelled the faint aroma of tobacco and ash and knew that he had been out for a cigarette. She had previously seen him in the garage lighting up and knew that if she needed him, it was a safe bet that Phillip would be there.

Phillip noticed Brianne's slight hesitation in her step as she passed him. He smiled to himself as he realized that she was taking in his masculine scent. He watched as she walked back to her office, then set about the task of preparing the conference room. He straightened the materials, laid out pads and pens for counsel and the audio recorder for the stenographer's later use.

Once he was satisfied with the room, Phillip picked up the phone and called the client. He had met him a number of times and had yet to grow even remotely fond of the man. Aside from his ability to marry spectacularly out of his league, which to look at him, one would know that it was the money that afforded him that ability, there was nothing admirable about him.

The complete lack of respect this man had for people he viewed beneath him was infuriating. Phillip listened as he berated his ex-wife, her counsel and himself. All of which, while vexing to listen to, was just par for the course with this abrasive jerk.

Phillip's hand flexed into a tight ball as he listened to their client's complaints. He closed his eyes against the imagery that played behind his lids. The wild fascinations he conjured all seemed to end with Phillip standing over his unmoving pudgy body.

The pencil Phillip held in his hand to take notes had snapped in half, the loud sound of the crack breaking his reverie. He ended the call and hung up the phone. He swept the shards of wood and lead off the table and replaced the pad he had been scribbling on.

He stepped out of the conference room. He needed to clear his head before that man stepped foot in the office.

Chapter Four

Litigation is an interesting beast. Parties try their best to appear unmovable, in order to negotiate from a position of strength, but it often isn't until they are face to face that the true drivers of the litigation are revealed.

In a divorce, it's almost always pride. Pride driven by hurt. And the wounded pride of a wealthy man can be hard to overcome, but when one resolves to attend to the hurt, pride, like most wounds, will heal.

Brianne began her interrogatories of her client's ex-wife.

"Now Gillian, can you remind us, how long had you been sleeping with the nanny?"

An easy question to get things started. And a cliché problem of the idle rich. Sleeping with the help. But the nanny? How salacious.

Red faces abound.

Sensing his discomfort, Brianne took her client outside and reminded him of the nature of the process.

Phillip straightened the knot in his tie and cast his eyes downward. The thick glass table revealed Gillian's athletic, tanned legs as she nervously crossed and uncrossed them. Her skin was a bronze color, her long wavy hair gathered to the side, hung over one shoulder.

She wore a navy-blue skirt suit with a cream blouse that did little to downplay her ample, and surgically augmented gifts. She had been, at one time, a very successful fitness instructor or life coach, Phillip hardly took the time to memorize the details anymore. She was stunning, though.

He pictured her in his mind, but in his mind, her hair was mussed, and she had an untamed look, almost wild. He brought his water glass to his lips and swallowed. He felt guilty. He only had those thoughts for Brianne. He needed to concentrate on the task at hand.

Their client, while also very successful in business, was a jowl-faced miser, which extended to both his money and his affections.

The one thing he seemed willing to spend his money on was to part with his trail of kept wives who all seemed to have a fidelity problem.

For whatever reason, this wife seemed to have gotten under the thick, jaundice tinged skin of their client and it was the impassioned antics in the hall that now captivated Phillip's attention.

Phillip watched the two of them through the glass walls; all the while refilling water pitchers and straightened pads and folders. Their conversation seemed to become heated as he noted the color rising in her cheeks and the way her manicured hands moved in short bursts.

Phillip felt his stomach tighten. He prepared himself to go into the hall to separate the two. He did not know what they were talking about, but he did not like the idea that anyone would speak to her in a manner that caused her to respond like that.

Phillip noted that Charles was also observing the not so discreet exchange from his office. He hoped Brianne could get control of the situation. Charles had quite a temper.

Something Brianne said must have appealed to the client's sensibilities because after a moment they came back into the room, and he was calm once more. An offer to negotiate terms of settlement of the dispute was put to the Respondent, which was reluctantly accepted and Brianne, a skillful negotiator, and with the guidance of her client, came to the table with a generous offer.

With the assistance of opposing counsel and a heavy dose of emotion from both sides of the table, the client and the Respondent in tears, counsel worked out a settlement that best suited the parties and would avoid a costly and unnecessary trial.

Charles lips formed into a tight smile as he watched Brianne's client walk toward the elevator. Their morning debrief would be very enlightening.

"That did not have to go to trial and now it won't," Brianne commented. Phillip helped her put the materials back into her office.

"Let's go out to celebrate," he said. Brianne always had hookups at the hottest clubs and with two screaming kids at home, it was the last place on earth Phillip wanted to be.

"Oh, I don't know Phil. Shouldn't you be getting home to those cute little ones?"

"Nah, Sara's got it under control. Besides, I feel like I am underfoot. Let's go to the new Cuban joint up the street."

Phillip married Sara Horner the same year Brianne had married Hugo. Sara had been one of the party girls Charles had entertained in his office once or twice that Phillip had called on for his own purposes later.

They had dated, but his true devotion was toward Brianne. When she married Hugo, it had upset him.

When Sara announced she was pregnant the first time he suspected that she hadn't been faithful, but he married her anyway. By the time the second kid came along, what had remained of her party girl good looks were gone.

Sara decided that she would stay home to care for the children. She decided. She sat around, ate, slept, and was a junkie. But she had always been a junkie. At least some things hadn't changed.

She had become more and more degrading over the years, and Phillip withdrew from her and toward his fantasy of Brianne and their imagined life together.

He hated Sara, her house and her kids. So, no, he had no desire to rush home to greasy-haired, sour-smelling children and an unkempt wife.

No. He would much rather have drinks with the well-manicured and freshly perfumed Brianne.

"Phil, I am sure she does not feel that way. She could probably use the help," Brianne continued.

"I am telling you that I am just in the way. Why can't you take me at my word? She can handle it!" Phillip's hands had tightened into fists at his side. Brianne sensed that it was no use to argue with him. It might be a good thing if he could go out for a drink and let off a little steam.

"You know what Phil, you are right. We should celebrate. We worked hard, and we deserve a drink. Let's pack this stuff up and get out of here." Brianne eyed him warily. She had known Phillip for several years and had only seen him angry a handful of times. Each time was frightening.

An easy smile came over his face, and he set about straightening the conference room. Phillip put the materials into the banker boxes he had brought in the room and carried them back to his desk. He straightened the stack of boxes in a tidy corner and turned off the lamp over his desk.

Brianne went back to her office to touch up her makeup, call her husband to let him know she would be going with Phillip for a quick drink after work and went to meet Phillip at the elevator.

In the garage, Phillip followed her to her door. "Are we going in one car?" Brianne asked.

"I thought we might as well. It's not very far, and we won't stay out too late. I can just walk back here and get my van or take a cab home."

Brianne thought that Phillip's rationale was a bit flawed, but if he was already thinking about how he would get to his car at the end of the night, she was fine with driving to the club.

Chapter Five

Upon their arrival, Phillip took her hand and led her to the bar. He ordered two vodka sodas and led her to a booth near the door to the kitchen where he talked about the vibrant feel of the club and the various states of undress of the young ladies in attendance. He was excited to be out with her. Though they had been out before, tonight was different. He felt it and knew she did too.

"Dance with me," he said and pulled her to her feet.

"Oh, I don't dance Phillip," she laughed.

"Come on. It'll be fun."

The Violence of Fire

Brianne followed him out on to the dance floor and they were swallowed by the sea of gyrating bodies. The Latin beats swelled over their bodies and pulsed into their very being.

Brianne lost sight of Phillip as she was swept away with the crowd. She let herself get caught up with the music and the people around her, letting go of the day. She was grateful to Phillip for making the suggestion. It was obvious that she needed it.

Her hair swayed around her shoulders, Brianne closed her eyes and allowed her other senses to overwhelm her. They painted a sensuous image. She felt her body moving to the music, caressing her, encouraging her to surrender.

Once separated, Phillip went to the bar and watched as Brianne danced unabashedly in the mass of sweaty bodies. He admired her willingness to give herself over to the excitement of the pulsating rhythm but felt jealousy overtake him as she moved amongst the crowd, and he saw the lustful glances of the men who bade her to dance with them.

He watched as she surrendered herself to the music, to them. The hairs on his arms stood on end as he watched the scene unfold. Her eyes were closed, and she was surrounded by admirers. Their bodies moved ever closer to her, closing his access to her.

Abigail Grimes

His hand closing tight on his glass, he snapped the hilt off the plastic sword that pierced his vodka-soaked olive, his eyes never leaving her. She did not seem to care how it made him feel; how she rejected him with every sway of her hip or sensuous movement of her lithe body. It was torture to watch her so free, knowing that she belonged to him. She should only feel that way when she was around him; when the day would come when she was in his arms.

Bitterly he finished his drink and went to seek her out. He couldn't take it anymore. Next time she would only dance with him.

He made his way to her on the dance floor. Moving with the music, he came up behind her. He slid his hand down the small of her back to her hip, leaning in to take in the smell of her perfume, his lips just a breath from her flesh. He planted his hand on the roundness of her hip firmly and turned her toward him.

Surprised, she stiffened and turned. Looking at him with caution, and with a gentle brush of her hand, she pushed his hand off her hip.

It was though she had slapped him in the face.

"Oh, I'm sorry. I didn't mean anything by it," he said, pulling his hand away. "It's just getting kind of late. I thought we had better be going," he said. Embarrassed tension bloomed between them.

Glancing at her watch, Brianne noted that it was nearing midnight. "Oh! You are right. Sorry about that. It was just a little unexpected," she said, looking at his balled fist hanging at his side.

Relaxing his hand, he gestured to the door and followed her outside.

"Do you need a lift back to the office to get your car?"

"Nah," Phillip replied. "It's a nice night, and it's not too far. I'll just walk."

"Are you sure? It's no trouble."

"I'm sure. You have quite a drive ahead of you. You should go on ahead."

"Thanks for tonight. I really needed to shake off a little steam. I'm glad you suggested it." Brianne wrapped her arms around him in a warm embrace. "I'll see you tomorrow."

With that, Brianne got into her car and drove off toward the highway.

Phillip watched her taillights fade into the distance, and he headed back to the office. His pulse was still in tune with the thumping rhythm of the club. He licked his lips and flexed his hands open and closed as fell in step with the flow of people out for the evening.

Her perfume lingered in his mind. The night had not gone how he had hoped. She had been hot and cold to him all night and so willing to let the hands of strangers caress her. Why not his hands? But how she held him when they said goodbye. The way her body molded to his own when she embraced him.

He felt swallowed whole by her affections. But now she was heading back to the countryside. Back to the carpenter. He fiddled with the Zippo in his pocket. He had to do something to get her off his mind.

His mind sparked with possibilities. He needed to relieve the tension.

Chapter Six

The night was busy. Most nights in the city were busy. Tourists bustling from event to event, night owls convinced that something exciting awaited them if they only stayed out long enough. Sometimes the exciting thing is the very thing you do not want to find. Someone would learn that lesson the hard way tonight.

***

Phillip walked down the bustling sidewalk, fishing a cigarette from his jacket. Standing under the streetlamp, one of the ladies who worked that particular corner approached him.

"Need a light?" she asked. Her perfume was nauseating.

"That'd be great. Thanks."

Phillip watched her fingers work the Bic. She was skinny and young. She probably hadn't been out here working long.

"How much for an hour?" he asked.

Licking his lips, he watched as she tilted her teenaged face to him — the streetlamp illuminating her face, accentuating the dark circles beneath her eyes.

"Depends. What you want me to do?" She smiled at him.

"How about we go for a walk, and we can negotiate a fair price for your services."

With that, he took her elbow and gently turned her toward the street.

They had been walking in silence for a few minutes when he stopped. He pulled a $100 bill out of his wallet and showed it to her.

"This is yours after we go for our little walk." He raised his hands to show her he meant no harm. "All I want to do is go for a little bit of a walk with some company. Deal?"

"What's your name?" she asked, suddenly very nervous. She rubbed her chewed fingernails along her long arms.

"My name is Phillip."

He smiled at her as he considered her thought process. He imagined that she reasoned he wouldn't have told her his name if he were a psychopath or something. Kids.

"Okay. Deal. My name is Trina." She smiled to herself as she thought of the warm night's sleep a hundred bucks could afford her.

Phillip guided her through the streets as they wound through parts of the city that grew less and less inhabited. He could sense her growing insecurity, so he took the bill from his wallet and handed it to her.

A crooked smile split her face as she took the money. Folding it in four, she placed it in the pocket of her denim skirt.

Trina didn't say much along the route. She listened to him tell her about his two kids and his vulture of a wife. Men are strange creatures, she thought. They were simple and desperate. This guy has two kids and a wife at home, and he's out here in the middle of the night with her. He wanted to talk, and that was fine.

A hundred bucks is a hundred bucks, and tonight she didn't have to earn it on her back. Not bad.

Chapter Seven

They came upon a park along a bike trail, and Phillip suggested they stop and talk on the bench. The bench sat in a quiet corner, and a small shallow stream trickled along the path.

It was a nice evening. Not too cool, and it was peaceful. The stream and the crickets were the evening's accompanying symphony. She took a deep breath and for the first time since they met, relaxed.

Trina sat on the bench, and Phillip stood before her. He smiled at her condescendingly. The rasp of his zipper filled the night.

"Well. Go on," he chided.

With a disappointed sigh, Trina set about to earn her living.

The Violence of Fire

"You should have seen her today," he sighed. "She was magnificent. The way she handled that asshole in the office. The way she got those rich idiots to agree and get out of our lives forever. She's amazing."

Phillip's eyes were closed as he recalled watching Brianne in action.

"Who are you talking about?" Trina questioned

Phillip stared down at her, eyes emblazoned with rage, and struck her across the cheek.

Grasping a fistful of auburn hair, he dragged her off the bench.

Tears blurred her eyes as Trina lifted her hands in submission. "I'm sorry. I'm sorry. Please don't," she pleaded.

He slapped her again. "Her name is Brianne. She is beautiful and brilliant. She is everything you're not."

His explanation was punctuated by the repeated connection of his hand to her face.

Trina tried to shield her face from his vicious assault. Her lip split and with blood from her eyebrow dripping steadily into her eye, he relented.

Regarding her with pity, he said, “Oh dear. Let’s clean you up a bit. You have made a bit of a mess.”

Phillip gently pushed Trina toward the stream.

Raw panic coursed through her. The metallic flavor of blood filled her mouth. Nausea overtook her, and she turned to run. She felt his arm close around her neck as he pulled her to his body. He was stronger than he looked, but she fought.

Phillip pulled her leg out from beneath her, and they fell to the ground. The musk of his skin, having saturated his shirt, drowned out the cheap flowers of her perfume. With one hand clasped over her mouth and the other tangled in her long hair, he dragged her to the stream. Gaining leverage, he placed his knee in her back, pressing her to the ground, her face just over the bank.

Leaning forward, he pushed her face into the seven inches of gurgling brook. Her body thrashed beneath him as she fought.

Trina sputtered in the water and tried her best to wrest him off her. Exhausted and overpowered, she felt herself slipping away. Brianne the brilliant. Her lungs burned. Why me? Why not you. Her last thought an echo along the current in the shallow creek; will anyone miss me?

The Violence of Fire

Phillip sat on the bank of the stream, watching Trina's hair move in the water. Her clothes had become disheveled in the struggle. Phillip slipped her denim skirt over her hips and down her legs taking care to reclaim his hundred-dollar bill. He removed her remaining clothes, folded them neatly and placed them beside him on the grass.

He played with the lighter while he sat on the bank. He did not want to rush this part. Watching the flash of the spark as the flame threatened to burst to life, he smiled. Trina should see this, he thought. Reaching for her, he pulled her face from the water and set her clothes alight.

Watching as the flames danced their destruction, the heat of his body rivaling that of the burning denim, he brought himself to the point of no return. A kaleidoscope of images crashed in his mind that he could no longer control. With a violent shudder, he released his excitement.

Sated, he stroked Trina's cheek and rolled her naked body into the stream.

***

Returning to the office, Phillip showered, changed his clothes and lay down on the couch in Brianne's office, where he left all thoughts of Trina and her nauseating perfume behind.

As Brianne pulled off her jacket, she gave a passing thought to Phillip and hoped that he got home alright. She locked the door and retired to the peace of her house.

Chapter Eight

The morning meeting was brief and loud. Brianne was called into Charles' office the next morning to outline the details of the settlement she had negotiated and to read her the riot act for the behavior she and the client had carried on with in the hallway the previous day. Brianne took her lumps and headed back to her office.

There was an odor she couldn't quite place in the room. It smelled of ash from her fireplace. She thought it odd but gave it no real consideration having decided that she must have tossed a sweater she had worn on the couch that she had on when they had a fire.

Around noon Phillip poked his head into her office and told her that he would be stepping out for a little while. Brianne nodded her consent and turned her attention back to her file. She trusted Phillip and knew he would be responsible with his time. Besides, if she needed anything, she knew he would drop whatever he happened to be doing and would return to the office.

Phillip got into his car and made his way to his modest three-bedroom townhouse. His wife would be there, and he would have to explain why he didn't come home last night. He did not look forward to that conversation. Pulling into the garage, he tossed his smoke-filled clothes into his gym bag and left the windows wound down a little bit to air out the car.

Inside the house, he could hear the TV in the family room. His youngest son's cries competed with the volume of the television. The door from the garage led to the laundry room, and once inside he opened the washer, tossed in the contents of his gym bag and turned on the machine.

He looked up to see his wife Sara standing in the doorway of the laundry room.

"Where the hell were you last night?" she demanded.

"Come on, Sara. Give me a break. You know how it is." Phillip looked beyond her as though she were a small annoyance.

The Violence of Fire

“I know how it is? What kind of an explanation is that?” She cocked her head to the side. “You have me sitting here like a chump waiting for your sorry ass to come home and give me a hand with these kids. You don’t even have the decency to call.” Her nasal voice rose an octave as she continued.

It was always the same argument. Phillip tired of her and her insipid demands. He envisioned wrapping his hands around her throat and squeezing; watching her face change from ruddy pink to scarlet.

To feel her chest hitch and hear her lungs rasp as she struggled to draw breath. The sheer terror in her eyes as she’d come to realize who is really in charge. Her submission would come too late of course, and he would leave her on the laundry room floor, her eyes fixed, unseeing at the cheap stucco above. He smiled.

“Are you even listening to me? Why are you so utterly useless? I have no idea what Brianne sees in you. You can’t follow simple instructions. You can’t speak up when spoken to. You can’t even get it up! I don’t even know when the last time you were able to do even that! Utterly useless.”

Sara laughed, her tone unforgiving, “Maybe that’s what Brianne is using you for, ‘cause you sure ain’t able to perform here. Poor bitch.”

The mention of Brianne's name cut him to the quick. How dare she? Brianne was perfect. Not like the strutting cow that Sara was. Brianne was graceful and eloquent. She was respectable and beautiful. Nothing like the slovenly witch who stood before him now.

Phillip brushed passed her and went to the living room. The joint she was smoking was perched on the lip of the ashtray, and the remnants of the line she had snorted dusted the coffee table. Their two-year-old son sat on the floor watching the television, oblivious to the confrontation happening behind him.

"Nice Sara! What is this? With the baby right here?" He pointed to the table. "Clean this shit up!"

"Oh! You`ve found your balls then?" Sara laughed as she swiped her finger through the white powder and licked it. "How about this Phil. How about you leave. Go back to the office; to where everything is nice and neat. Back to your little girlfriend with the stick up her ass; where everything is just so. Just leave."

"She is not my girlfriend! But she could teach you a thing or two about being a woman. Look at you! You're a fucking mess."

"I'm a mess? Have you looked in a mirror lately? You're a joke, Phil. And you're right. She isn't your girlfriend. She's your boss. She wouldn't stoop so low as to be with a spineless piece of shit such as yourself. You're pathetic. You idealize a woman who tells you when to sit, when to stand and when to shit. I hope to God that these boys grow a pair and can one day teach you how to be a man." Turning her attention to the boy, she cooed, "But given their gene pool, there's not much hope. Right, baby? Where is your brother?"

The child looked up at his mother and smiled.

"Get out Phil. Go back to your master. Tell her hi for me." Sara lowered herself onto the couch and took a drag off her joint.

Enraged but impotent before her, Phillip stood beside the couch in silence. The older of his two children walked into the room. Not yet in pre-school, this one was a chatterbox. Curious and playful but he looked so much like Sara, it was difficult to like the boy.

Barely registering the child's absurd babbling, Phillip looked down at him. His little face tear-stained as he told his sorrowful tale about a toy he could not locate. Phillip patted his head and walked away.

Sara took a white pill from a plastic bag on the coffee table and crushed it with a spoon. Ketamine. She would be useless soon. As useless as she claimed he was.

Phillip smirked as he watched his wife fall into the K-hole. Her zombie-like stare directed at the television. When she was in that state, she couldn't move, couldn't talk. She claimed it was a hell of a trip, like an out of body experience.

He hadn't experienced it himself, having only snorted a bit of it once with her and some friends when they were first together. The sensation was not something he enjoyed. He liked control.

It was then that the thought occurred to him that having some 'Special K' available the next time would save him a bit of the trouble that he experienced with Trina the night before.

Taking a drag from Sara's joint, he picked up the bag that had the remaining pills and went to the kitchen. Turning the dial on the gas stove, he blew out the pilot light and took a last look at the pitiful souls in the living room.

He pocketed the bag and left the way he came in. He knew that when Sara came to, she would immediately reach for her lighter, and that would be the end of that problem. At least the kids would be sleeping, he thought.

Maybe Sara had been right. Brianne did need him, and he needed her. She was his girlfriend. He backed out of the garage and directed himself back to the office to start his life, baggage free.

Chapter Nine

Brianne sat in her office, staring at the file on her desk. She would have to give the material to Phillip to compile the motion for filing with the court. Having reviewed her opponent's affidavit, she knew that she had to rethink her strategy.

She got up from her chair and stretched her back. Standing at the window, she looked down to the street below. She wanted to go out and be part of the action. The city was always so alive. She felt a twinge of jealousy as she watched the people below.

Charles watched her from the door of her office. He loved the swing of her hips as she moved. How natural she was, how effortlessly seductive. He cleared his throat as she bent at the waist to stretch her back. He didn't want her to see him standing there unannounced.

Her eyes had caught Charles' reflection in the window when he had first positioned himself in the doorway. She had pretended not to know he was there as she did not need him to treat her any worse than he already did. Charles had a way of making his female employees very uncomfortable under his gaze.

His predatory stare ran over her body and eventually found her eyes. "Do you have that trademark decision I asked you to find? I would like to review the entire file. Did you bring it in today?"

"Hi Charles, yes. I have the file. It's in my car. I will go down and get it."

"That's what we have assistants for, dear. Where is Phil anyway?" Charles eyebrow arched.

"Oh, I sent him to run an errand for me. He should be back any time now."

Brianne's eyes moved passed her boss' shoulder to Phillip's desk. Where was he? He's been gone for nearly an hour.

"If you need it now, I can go get it for you. But if it can wait, I will get Phillip to retrieve it when he gets back."

"It's fine. When he gets in, have him bring it to me."

His eyes lingered on her form for an uncomfortable moment before he turned to leave.

Shaking her head, she picked up the phone to call Phillip.

Phillip had been down the hall watching Charles leering at Brianne. His Brianne. The man was a predator.

It was a poorly held secret in the office that Charles was a womanizer. He was inappropriate to the female staff at all levels, but it was also the culture in the office that if you were female and you wanted to excel, you had to hold your nose and go along with his chauvinistic tendencies.

As a man in the office, you were just expected to work hard and stay away from whomever Charles had set his sights on.

This would not stand. Brianne was not the type to pander to Charles' advances. And even if the thought crossed her mind, Phillip would not allow her to fall under Charles' influence.

His phone began to ring as he approached her office. Glancing down at the caller ID, he smiled. She did need him. Instead of answering the phone,

Phillip stuck his head in her office. "Hey, what's up?"

Brianne had her office telephone in her hand, but her cell phone to her ear. He took a step into her office and was stopped short by a look.

She looked at him with minor annoyance and pointed to a slip of paper on her desk.

He cocked his head, confused by the tone of the room. He was here to help her after all, what was her problem? He approached her desk to retrieve the note and stood before her waiting for any additional instructions.

"Hang on a second, Honey," Brianne said into the phone. She covered the microphone and glared at Phillip. "Charles was in here a minute ago. He's gonna have my ass if I don't give him that file. Where have you been?" The anxiety in her voice was palpable.

Stepping toward her, Phillip reached his hand for hers. She stepped away and waved him out of her office.

"Oh," she called after him. "Here are my keys. The file is in the trunk. Just grab it and bring it back up here. And hurry!"

She tossed the keys toward him and went back to her phone call. They landed on the floor a foot from where he stood.

Phillip looked at the keys laying on the ground and thought of Sara. How she belittled him, how she said that Brianne just used him, that he was no more than her errand boy. He could feel his cheeks flush with fury as he stooped to retrieve the keys.

"Phillip is sitting on the floor of my office for some reason." Her conversation seeping through the echoing rage thrashing in his mind. "I asked him to go get something for me, but for some reason I can still see him."

He looked up at her. Her eyebrows were arched arrogantly. He wanted to slap that look off her face. What was wrong with her today? And why today?

After all the wonderful things he had said about her. All the things that he had done for her. How could she? He loved her. He rose to his feet and left.

Immediately regretful, Brianne confessed to Hugo. "Damnit. I think I really pissed him off. I haven't seen that look on his face before. I can't even describe it. It was like a mix of anger and hurt. I don't know. I was out of line. I have to make it up to him. I'll take him for a drink after work to apologize, but I won't be late tonight. I promise."

Phillip opened the trunk to Brianne's sedan and set the boxes on the ground. He went around to the driver's side and opened the door. Reaching below the steering wheel, he pulled the release for the hood. He gazed at the mechanics of her magnificent vehicle. He wanted to tear it all out the way she tore out his heart. How she treated him like a mere servant. Someone to pick up after her, like an afterthought. He toyed with the lead to the fuel pump fuse but thought better of it. There was no point in damaging such a fine vehicle when it was she who was the problem.

Phillip went to his car and pocketed the bag of Ketamine.

"Hey, Phillip." Brianne looked up from the transcript on her desk. "Listen, I am really sorry about earlier. I was way out of line. Charles got under my skin and then Hugo called, and we got into it a bit, and I took it out on you. I apologize."

The meek smile on her lips, and humility in her eyes conveyed her sincerity.

Phillip was taken aback by the apology. "I will put the boxes in the conference room." He said. "I can tell Charles that they are in there for you. You don't have to talk to him about it again." His emotions were confused by the kindness.

"Thanks, Phillip. I appreciate that. He can be a lot to deal with. And clearly, I have enough to deal with as it stands," Brianne said as she motioned to the various piles of paper strewn across her desk.

Smiling, Phillip cringed at the mess. How he wished he could straighten those piles.

"I know. You can't wait until I leave for the day so you can tidy this up, huh?" she laughed. "Well, that won't be today because we are cutting out early. That call I got from Hugo earlier was to remind me that we would be having company this weekend and that we have to get the house in tip-top shape," Brianne said rolling her eyes. "I told him that I would be home on time tonight, but I also said that I wanted to take you out for a drink. If you are willing, of course."

"Sure. That sounds like a great idea. I would love to go for a drink with you tonight." Phillip beamed.

He would get to be alone with her again. Dance with her again. He was very much looking forward to it.

"How about you toss that stuff in the conference room, I'll pack up in here, and we cut out for the rest of the day?" She stretched her arms over her head and sought under her desk for her pumps.

Phillip watched her painted toes pull the shoes closer to her, and the long line of her legs flex as she slipped them on. Excited, he took the boxes to the conference room. On his way back to his desk he passed by Charles' office and advised him of the location of the files.

"Where the hell have you been?" Charles demanded.

"Oh, Chuck. My boss had me run a couple of errands for her. Don't worry. Brianne and I are going to step out for the rest of the day. We have some important business to attend to. And Chuck, we all see the way you look at her. It's wholly inappropriate, and I won't stand for it any longer. She's taken. What exactly do you not understand about that? Back off." Phillip winked at Charles and closed the door.

Charles sputtered with anger. How dare Phillip speak to him in that manner? Charles picked up the phone to call Brianne into his office. The phone rang through to Phillip's desk where it went straight to his voicemail. Charles slammed the phone into its cradle and glared at the closed door.

Phillip walked down the hall, threaded Brianne's arm through the crook in his and they left the office behind.

In the parking garage, Phillip directed them towards her car. "Do you mind if we take your car again?" he asked.

"Not at all. You really like this car, huh?" Brianne opened the doors, and they climbed in. "I do too. I bought it when I first joined the firm."

Brianne talked about the car like it was a member of the family. Suddenly embarrassed under Phillip's gaze, Brianne said. "We can only go for a quick drink. I can't be late tonight."

Pulling the car into the mid-day traffic, Brianne drove off in the direction of the Cuban restaurant they had attended earlier.

"I really liked that place last night. Do you mind if we go back there?"

Phillip smiled. "Not at all."

It was their place. Pulling his phone out of his pocket, he noted the time. He had left his old life behind an hour ago, and already things were going so well. Turning off his phone he turned in his seat and let his eyes take in Brianne's profile. He did not want anything to interrupt the true beginning of his life.

***

Across town, an explosion ripped through Phillip's townhouse complex.

An unfortunate result of the combination of Sara's ketamine dulled senses, natural gas, and her need to relight the joint on the coffee table.

She didn't notice that the children lay unconscious on the floor. She had simply been pleased that they were quiet for once.

The oxygen surrounding the lighter was digested by the tiny spark and the blaze expanded outward, engulfing the room in a violent burst of light.

Flames, like excited nymphs, reached out their arms seeking new paths to satisfy their appetite. Thick ropes of black smoke billowed angrily into the sky.

The destruction absolute.

Chapter Ten

The parking lot was busy at that time of day, but Brianne found parking somewhat close to the door. Inside, the restaurant was quite dark already. It had a sultry quality even at 4 o'clock in the afternoon.

Phillip went to the bar and ordered drinks for them as Brianne sought out a table. It was strange to her that there were so many patrons in the bar. The lighting subdued, the music was almost carnal.

Setting the drinks down, Phillip and Brianne discussed the current case and the upcoming motion before the court.

The conversation became more personal as the topic turned to Charles and his treatment of the staff. Phillip reached his hand across the table and patted Brianne's hand as she told him what some of the staff were saying.

Though it made her somewhat uncomfortable, Brianne smiled at Phillip's gesture. She did not need his condolences.

"I told him off for you," Phillip beamed.

"You what?" Brianne pulled her hand back then. "What do you mean you told him off? And for me?"

"Yeah, I see how he looks at you. I told him that you were taken and that he should back off." Phillip smiled at her, proud that he stood up for her to the senior partner.

"What the hell, Phillip? He's probably going to try to have us fired! Think about what you just did. You have a wife and kids! That was not smart."

"I'm not too worried about that. It will all work out. I promise." Phillip reached for her hand again.

The vibration and chime of Brianne's cell phone drew her focus away from the strange light in Phillip's eyes. She shook her head, unable to believe what she just heard and picked up the phone.

"Hi, Babe." Brianne turned away from Phillip and concentrated on the phone. "I'm almost done here. I will be on my way soon."

Phillip understood that Brianne was upset with him, but knew that if he could explain himself, she would understand. Even be grateful to him.

He had protected her. Charles was dangerous. And Hugo was disruptive. He was always popping up, interrupting their private moments. He would no longer tolerate the disruptions.

Phillip called the waitress over and ordered bottle service. He and Brianne would enjoy their first date.

The waitress brought a bottle of vodka to their table along with a carafe of cranberry juice, and they watched the parade of people pass by entwined in an intricate and erotic dance. Her phone call with Hugo seemed to him very one-sided, with only the occasional acknowledgment on Brianne's part.

Listening to their inane conversation and her profession of love to him pushed him into action. He could not share her with anyone else.

He wouldn't.

Phillip pulled one of the ketamine tablets from his jacket pocket and slipped it under his glass. While Brianne was distracted, he crushed it and dusted the powder into his hand. Fixing her a cocktail, Phillip dosed the glass and slid it across the table.

"Listen, Phillip. I have to get going. We can talk about this Charles situation in the morning. Hugo really needs me home. It's a long drive, so I have to go."

"I just ordered these drinks. You aren't going to make me sit here alone and drink them, are you?" he pouted at her.

He would not be cuckolded by a carpenter. Brianne was his now.

She thought his behavior strange but agreed to have one final drink with him.

He insisted that they toast. She didn't ask him what he meant by the new chapter in his life. She was already thinking of being home with Hugo. Making love in front of a roaring fire, wrapped in his arms.

She finished the drink in several quick swallows. Assessing herself to determine her sobriety, she began to register an uneasiness.

Brianne watched Phillip as he spoke to her in his animated state and slowly began to realize that she was no longer able to process what he was saying.

Phillip was changing before her eyes. Panic had set in. What had he done? Had he drugged her? There was no other explanation. But why?

"Please," Brianne pleaded. Her voice just a whisper, her mouth cottony. "Please, Phillip. Let me go home." She had to focus her concentration to form the words. She felt a serious disconnect within her body.

His smile grew wider, distorting his face, twisting into a terrifying sneer. He closed his hand over hers as she attempted to grasp for her purse. Her coordination was off. She couldn't understand why she couldn't get her hands to cooperate, why her limbs failed to respond to her brain's commands.

Phillip reached for her purse which lay on the seat beside her and took her keys, then placing her weight against his shoulder, Phillip lifted Brianne to her feet. Steadying her against his body, he looked like a gentleman helping his lover who had indulged in one too many.

Satisfied that no one was watching him with much interest, he led her out to the parking lot. He placed her in the passenger seat and got behind the wheel of the car that he had dreamed of for so long.

Checking to see that she was still breathing, Phillip put the car in gear and eased out of the parking lot. He drove through the city for a while, enjoying his joyride.

He talked to Brianne along the way, telling her how much he loved the powerful engine and the feel of the road and thanking her for the opportunity to take it for a spin. He laughed then. A cruel sound. She stared out windshield, her body limp, a tear spilled over her cheek.

He parked the car on a side street just off the busy thoroughfare. She could hear the laughter and excitement in the air. The city was abuzz. He walked around to the passenger side and pulled her out onto the concrete.

She was screaming. Why wasn't anyone coming to help her? Her voice had failed her. All those jovial people just 100 feet away. Would no one come down this street? Would no one see what this monster was doing?

Phillip finally had his moment with her; to make her understand how she made him feel. He stood on the precipice of mania and desire and felt himself topple. The power, the control that he felt as she sat crumpled at his feet. It was intoxicating.

He began to scream at her. He told her that she was nothing without him, that he knew that she tried to seduce him. He slapped her then. He told her that she would not return to Hugo. He explained to her that he wouldn't submit to her tricks any longer. She was his now. Blow after blow he rained down upon her as his lecture continued.

He tore her clothes from her body, as though he were possessed. He pulled a flask from his jacket and soaked her clothes. Lighting a cigarette, he explained to her that he knew that his wife thought he was a screw-up. That she had convinced herself that the two of them were having an affair. A knowing smile curled his lips and confided that she would not be a problem for them anymore.

He put the cigarette on the pile of clothes and watched as it caught. Recalling the feeling of ecstasy while watching Trina, Phillip turned Brianna's face to the dancing embers. He watched the reflection of the flames dance and flash in her eyes as the hungry flames devoured the delicate garments.

That laugh again. It threatened to break her. The smoke rose in angry plumes. She watched as he torched her clothes, afraid that he would spill the remnants of the flask on her skin and watch in morbid fascination as the flames lapped at her naked body.

Phillip stared down at her as though she were nothing. His thoughts were chaotic. He loved her. Idolized her. She was so far above him. But now she lay before him, much as Trina had. A whore. She would submit to him. He would possess her.

She watched as he pulled her legs apart. His eyes devoured her. Humiliated her. Her thighs fell to the side, revealing the most intimate parts of her to his violating touch. She fought to regain control, to move her limbs, to stop him. Whatever he had given her left her defenseless. All that remained was to watch as he opened his belt and exposed himself, readying himself to take her.

He entered her then. His sweat-beaded brow mere inches from hers as the grave defilement carried on. Spittle rained down upon her vulnerable form as he belittled at her. He turned her tear-stained face to look him and kissed her on her bloodied lips. Restraining her with horrifying dominance, the abuse continued.

When he was finished, he pushed her to the side like a child no longer amused with a toy.

Brianne had tried to go somewhere else in her mind, but every strike from his hand kept her attention in each sickening moment. He was still. She could barely turn her head to see him. He sat away from her. He was clothed. He was even wearing his jacket. He drank from the flask, spilling alcohol on himself in the process.

He appeared to be crying. How dare you cry you bastard? She silently screamed. A strangled sound escaped her throat.

Phillip turned to her and appraised her filthy body. Rising to his feet, he picked her up and placed her back in the car.

"Time to get you home," he said.

She tried in vain to strike out at him. To throw herself back on the ground. She knew she would have a better chance if she could just regain some control.

He buckled her in and smoothed her hair. Smiling down at her, he closed the door, walked around to the driver's side, and slid behind the wheel.

"I do love this car," he sighed as he pulled back out into the flow of traffic.

Tears flowed down her cheeks. She stared at the crowded streets. Why didn't any of you help me? Couldn't you hear me? Her chest racked with sobs.

He pulled around to the office and parked the car in the garage. He leaned over.

"I'm sorry about all that," he said, waving his hand dismissively. He kissed her forehead. "I love you, Brianne. I'll see you tomorrow."

Leaving the keys in the car, he closed the door, walked twenty feet to his minivan, and drove away.

Home to his family, she thought. Oh, Sara.

The stabbing prickle of the return of sensation lit her skin ablaze. She began to cry in earnest.

Chapter Eleven

Phillip drove to the beach. He watched the ebb and flow of the tide. It soothed him. Night had fallen, and the beach was all but deserted.

They had finally consummated their relationship. Phillip smiled. He was happy. He had shown her the depth of his feelings. He told her how he truly felt about her.

Phillip fished his cigarettes out of his pocket. The remaining ketamine pills were dragged out alongside the packet. He examined them for a moment and lit a cigarette. Replaying the moments in his mind, he saw Brianne smiling at him under the lights at the restaurant, her long legs under her desk. Legs now covered in scratches and bramble. He shook his head.

Was that how it happened? A lazy trickle of water, red hair dancing in a stream, the sound of glasses clinking. The images swirled together in a confusing mess in his mind. Denim. The pair arm in arm. The smell of sweat and cheap perfume. Phillip looked at the remaining pills. He was confused. He was convinced that they had shared a wonderful moment, but something plagued him. Why had she been crying? He looked to the rearview mirror for answers.

Could it be that he forced himself on her? He could never have done that. Not to her pristine delicate body. It was a temple. Sacred. He would never desecrate the only thing he ever truly loved. It couldn't be. She didn't fight.

He explained why things had turned out the way they did. He knew she would understand how deep his feelings were for her. He vowed to find her tomorrow to explain. She would understand. And the next time she would submit willingly.

He shifted his gaze away from the mirror. He could no longer face the true nature of what he had done. He wanted to commune with her, to feel what she felt, if just for a moment. He swallowed the pills.

The Violence of Fire

He wanted to get home, having forgotten that he no longer had a home to which he could return. He put the van in drive and eased off the brake. He expected the ketamine to sweep a euphoric sensation through him. The realization came too late that it was but a tomb for the living. He fought the K-hole as it approached; the car rolling slowly forward as he sunk further into the zombie-like state.

The cigarette in his mouth dropped from its perch and landed on his alcohol-soaked jacket. The eruption of flames almost immediate. He screamed in terror. Only no sound came, his mouth agape.

Unable to move his body, he could only watch. The allure of the fire as it encompassed his body captivated his attention until they no longer registered in his mind. His sightless eyes affixed to the mirror, reflecting the horror.

Epilogue

A car pulled up beside hers. How long had she been here? Had Phillip returned? Her panic grew exponentially. Brianne began to scream. Had he returned to kill her, to finish what he had started in that dirty alley?

It had been hours since they had last spoken. Hugo had tried to call Brianne several times, and after leaving numerous messages, he checked her location on his cell phone. Confused by the fact that she was still at work and afraid of the implications of what it might mean if she was no longer responding to his calls, he traveled to her office.

Hugo pled with building security to allow him access to the garage and insisted that they call for help. And now, at her closed door, he knew that she was alive, but he also knew that there were worse things than what he had envisioned.

Through the window, Hugo tried to comfort her. He tried to let her know that she was safe, that help would arrive shortly. He attempted to open the door, and she screamed. She locked the door. It was all she could do to protect herself.

Her face smeared with blood and her body naked and bruised, Hugo could barely control his rage, his despair. Seeing her so afraid made him afraid. She would not hold his gaze. He wanted to hold her. He sat down on the ground with his head in his hands and waited for the ambulance to arrive.

Brianne sat propped up in her hospital bed and listened as the police explained that Phillip's charred remains had been driven into the lake. They noted that it did not seem that he had attempted to escape the vehicle. She remembered the terror she felt when she lost control of her body. She wondered if they thought that this information would bring her some peace. It didn't. It only served to deepen the horror of the thing. And now she was left with nothing. Nothing but her thoughts.

She played back the sickening moments in her mind again and again. She brought her hands to her chest and squeezed them together. She did that often. She had to make sure she still had control.

He violated her. In time her body would heal, but it was what he stole from her that was worse. The smell of the fire, the splash of light on the cityscape, the bustle of the downtown streets at night. He had stolen those things from her. She would never again experience them the same way. They were no longer comforts. They were now part of her waking nightmare.

Hugo sat at her bedside. He was very still, as though he were made of stone. He was wary of making any sudden movements. He did not want to upset her. But it was the stillness that unsettled her. And how could he know that? He looked at her as though she might break at any moment.

She watched him as he looked at her. She felt as if she were on display behind glass. They were so close, but there was a divide; the distance too great. She wondered if there was a deeper evil inside of him. She didn't believe there was, but she wasn't sure anymore.

He had stopped reaching for her hand. She would only pull it away when he tried. She felt that she would trust him again. Touch him again — one day. But for now, she could just watch and hope.

The End

Acknowledgments

Thank you to the friends and family who helped me get this story off the laptop and into the real world.

Thank you especially to Taina Wong, Nadine Hurmal, and Vanessa George, who were the beta readers for this story. You are wonderful human beings, and your feedback was invaluable.

Thank you to Diana Grimes for being excited about this story. Your encouragement means so much. I am so glad you came to visit!

Thank you to Anil Kamal. You are a tough critic, but I know my work is always safe in your thoughtful hands. It is a gift to have an editor who is also a close friend.

Thank you to my dear friend Garnet Morgan for allowing me into your office to rant about this or that. It has helped clear space in my head more times than you will ever know.

And finally, thank you to my husband, Kevin Matthew, for giving me formatting advice and I.T. assistance. Your ongoing support, both emotional and technical is immeasurable. Thanks for just being you.

About the Author

Abigail Grimes is the author of stories that range from bone-tingling thrillers and gripping fiction to poetry and non-fiction with heart.

She works in the bustling metropolitan city of Toronto, Ontario and loves to write and relax at her home in rural Ontario, where she lives with her husband.

www.abigailgrimes.com

Manufactured by Amazon.ca
Acheson, AB